✿Paisley Atoms✿

KITCHEN CHAOS

By J.L. Anderson

Illustrated by Alan Brown

Rourke
Educational Media
rourkeeducationalmedia.com

www.rourkeeducationalmedia.com

Edited by: Keli Sipperley
Cover and Interior layout by: Rhea Magaro-Wallace
Cover and Interior Illustrations by: Alan Brown

Library of Congress PCN Data

Kitchen Chaos / J.L. Anderson
(Paisley Atoms)
ISBN (hard cover)(alk. paper) 978-1-68191-719-1
ISBN (soft cover) 978-1-68191-820-4
ISBN (e-Book) 978-1-68191-915-7
Library of Congress Control Number: 2016932597

Printed in the United States of America,
North Mankato, Minnesota
01-0162313009

Dear Parents and Teachers,

Future world-famous scientist Paisley Atoms and her best friend, Ben Striker, aren't afraid to stir things up in their quests for discovery. Using Paisley's basement as a laboratory, the two are constantly inventing, exploring, and, well, making messes. Paisley has a few bruises to show for their work, too. She wears them like badges of honor.

These fast-paced adventures weave fascinating facts, quotes from real scientists, and explanations for various phenomena into witty dialogue, stealthily boosting your reader's understanding of multiple science topics. From sound waves to dinosaurs, from the sea floor to the moon, Paisley, Ben and the gang are perfect partner resources for a STEAM curriculum.

Each illustrated chapter book includes a science experiment or activity, a biography of a woman in science, jokes, and websites to visit.

In addition, each book also includes online teacher/parent notes with ideas for incorporating the story into a lesson plan. These notes include subject matter, background information, inspiration for maker space activities, comprehension questions, and additional online resources. Notes are available at: www.RourkeEducationalMedia.com.

We hope you enjoy Paisley and her pals as much as we do.

Happy reading,
Rourke Educational Media

Table of Contents

Chapter One
Bake Sale Surprise

"I have a big surprise!" Mrs. Proton, the school principal, said during morning announcements.

The entire fifth grade at Roarington Elementary chattered.

"Think we're going to have a bonus science fair?" Paisley whispered to Ben.

"Doubtful. Maybe we'll get out of school early. That will give us some extra lab time," Ben replied.

Extra lab time would be awesome, though Paisley secretly hoped Roarington Elementary would have another science fair. This year's was epic.

"I'm sure Mrs. Proton is going to brag about my recent spelling bee win," Whitney-Raelynn said.

Paisley clenched her teeth together to keep herself from saying something she might regret. In her mind, Whitney-Raelynn won by default. Paisley and Ben had to skip the spelling bee to help Paisley's mom with an adventure.

Paisley might've been great at science and math, but she was a good speller and had been practicing. Ben had even better odds of winning the spelling bee—fourteen percent more likely according to his calculations.

"Are you pregnant?" Arjun asked Mrs. Proton.

Mrs. Proton laughed. "Goodness, no, but I did become a grandma recently. The surprise is that we'll be getting some new science equipment."

Rosalind reclined in her wheelchair on the back two wheels and then popped forward, cheering.

"Calm down," Mrs. Proton said. "Don't get too excited yet because each grade level will need to participate in some fund-raising. There will be a fifth grade bake sale at the PTA meeting, and to add some excitement, there will be a prize given for the best treat."

"I'm going to win another award at Roarington Elementary! But first, I'm going to take home the city spelling bee trophy!" Whitney-Raelynn said, looking right at Paisley with a smirk.

"We'll see about that," Paisley said, trying to think of the yummiest, most creative treat she could think of for the bake sale.

Mrs. Proton went over some of the bake sale rules, but Paisley was lost in thought. Her dad made amazing jalapeño cornbread, and Paisley and her mom went wild for his sweet potato biscuits with cumin and chili. Her stomach rumbled but she wanted to dream up something even more unique with Ben.

The fifth graders continued to buzz about the bake sale, and even Mrs. Beaker, their science teacher, gave them free time to brainstorm recipes.

"Cooking is all about chemistry," Mrs. Beaker said.

"Don't forget math," Paisley said. "Cooking involves a lot of measurement."

Mrs. Beaker huffed. "Of course it is all about math."

Paisley decided not to add health or anything else to the list so Mrs. Beaker wouldn't change her mind

about the free time.

"Depending on the amount of funds we raise, we'll be getting microscopes, beakers, and a super-powered telescope," Mrs. Beaker said.

Paisley could hear the excitement in her teacher's voice, which was saying a lot since Mrs. Beaker wasn't as wild about science as she was. Rumor had it that Mrs. Beaker wanted to teach math instead. Regardless, who wouldn't be excited about new equipment?

Roarington Elementary was an older school and it needed as much new equipment as possible. The pressure weighed heavily on Paisley.

The twins Suki and Sumi talked about making double-stacked peanut butter cookie sandwiches. Paisley thought about making something with peanuts to honor George Washington Carver. George Washington Carver was a botanist just like her mom and made all kinds of inventions. He was famous for dreaming up a variety of ways to use peanuts.

As much as she admired him, Paisley wanted to create something different than Suki and Sumi. Plus,

Arjun thought he might be allergic to peanuts. Peanut allergies could be really serious and she wanted to make something that would hopefully be safe for everyone to eat.

"We could make some clock-themed cupcakes," Ben said. He really loved making watches like his namesake Benjamin Banneker.

"We could, but I think we need something even more out of this world, Ben," Paisley said.

"I have a feeling your quest might lead us to somewhere wild," he said.

"I hope so," Paisley said with a grin.

If only she knew what to make for the bake sale! Paisley wanted to help the school, plus she wanted to keep Whitney-Raelynn from winning another award. There wasn't much Whitney-Raelynn wasn't good at. Even her name was an overachiever.

Ben walked home with Paisley after school and they both kept thinking about different treats but nothing seemed yummy or special enough.

Paisley's house smelled spicy when they walked

inside. Newton, her rescued pet mongoose, ran up Paisley's leg. "I missed you, too!" she said.

Dad was in the kitchen humming. He'd scattered measuring cups everywhere and the countertops looked sandy from sprinkles of cornmeal.

Paisley nearly jumped for joy. "Does all this cooking mean Mom is coming home?"

Dad always cooked a big meal whenever Mom returned after one of her many travels. She was currently in Mexico studying some plant species.

Dad shook his head no. "I wish, but she'll be home before we both know it. I'm making a dinner tonight to celebrate something."

Before Paisley or Ben could ask what the celebration was about, Dad left everything he was preparing and went to his office to retrieve a petri dish covered in a plastic case like those sports collectors used to display baseballs.

"This is what we're celebrating?" Paisley asked.

The petri dish was covered with goo that looked like mustard. Newton sniffed it and then perched on

Paisley's shoulders.

"Yes!" Dad said and did an air-guitar-playing happy dance. Dad was probably the only person Paisley knew who would get that pumped about a yucky looking petri dish.

"Before I forget, we could make pretzels for the bake sale," Ben said. He must've thought the goo looked like mustard, too.

"Yuck," Paisley said.

"Doesn't seem like either one of you are all that impressed," Dad said. He was still smiling. "Maybe this will change your mind. This is a bacteria specimen collected from a meteorite."

"Really?" Paisley leaned in for a closer look. Newton chattered in her ear.

It was hard to imagine that the goo came from a meteorite. Paisley couldn't wait to get a look at the petri dish under a microscope.

"A co-worker of mine sent the specimen to me," Dad said. "I think it is the coolest thing I've ever had in my collection."

Paisley looked around Dad's office. He was a biologist and had some pretty cool things like his scorpion collection and huge bones that might've belonged to Bigfoot.

"Since it came from a meteorite, is it an alien bacteria specimen?" Ben asked.

Paisley was off her game. She hadn't stopped to think about the meteorite being from outer space and the whole alien connection.

Dad rocked out again, grabbing one of the bones on display to use as a guitar this time. Paisley and Ben laughed.

"Do you find this *humerus*?" Dad asked. He put the bone down. "Now in all seriousness, I believe the bacteria is an indication of strange life signs from somewhere in the universe."

The house was warm from Dad's cooking, but this comment gave Paisley the chills.

She had a whole new level of respect for the mustard goo.

"Dinner is almost ready," Dad said. "I've made

vegetarian chili, and one of your favorites, Paisley. Jalapeño cornbread."

The day had gotten so much better! Paisley had been thinking about her dad's cornbread ever since the bake sale topic came up. She couldn't wait to eat and find out more information about the bacteria specimen.

Chapter Two
The Wonder of Bacteria

Paisley bit big chunks of cornbread and wished that Mom was with them. She would've been fascinated by the bacteria, too.

Newton chomped on an egg with a side of worms.

Ben helped himself to a second slice of cornbread. "Is this the first meteorite bacteria ever found?" Ben asked with his mouth full.

Dad shook his head. He was covered in cornbread batter and chili dribbles. "Scientists found some fossilized bacteria on meteorites in the past, sort of like pond scum."

Paisley looked out of the kitchen window into the evening sky wondering how much life there was out there in the universe.

As much she wanted to look at the mustard goo under the microscope after dinner, Paisley checked in with her mom first.

"See you in a little bit," Ben said. He went home to have dinner with his parents. Paisley had no idea how he could eat so much. Ben's parents worked from home designing bridges. They were as neat as Paisley and Ben were messy so they never minded the two of them spending a lot of time at the Atoms house.

While Paisley waited for her mom to connect to the video chat, she ran her hand over the ancient key her mother had given her when she was a little girl. Newton was perched on her neck and nudged her hand for attention.

"Hola, *mija*," Mom said after connecting. She had a white and yellow plumeria pushed behind her ear. It was a flower grown in Mexico. Paisley had also

seen lots of the same kind of flowers in Hawaii, where
Newton was rescued when he was injured as a baby.

Paisley told her mom all about Dad's bacteria specimen. Mom's eyes lit up. "Your dad sent me pictures. So exciting! Intergalactic exciting, in fact."

Paisley's mom and dad had so much in common. They were perfect for each other, and they were the perfect parents for her, too.

"Is everything okay, *mija*?" Mom asked.

Paisley wondered if her mom could tell how much she was missing her or how she was worried about the bake sale. She'd only mentioned the bacteria after all.

"I wished you could've been here with us tonight," Paisley said and told her mom all about the cornbread and chili. She decided to keep the bit about the messy kitchen to herself.

"Yum! I wish I could share my dessert with you," Mom said. She held her slice of tres leches cake up to the video camera. The cake, soaked in three kinds of milk, looked gooey and sweet.

Even if she was stuffed, Paisley could've pulled a Ben and eaten the entire slice it looked so delicious!

"Mom, you're a genius," Paisley said.

"Are you talking about the Mexican herbs I've been researching to cure the common cold?" Mom asked.

"No, but that is brilliant," Paisley said. "I'm talking about the tres leches cake. I wasn't sure what to make for the school bake sale. Now that's what I'm going to make, with a small twist."

"Sounds like a winner," Mom said.

When Ben came over after his second dinner, he wasn't so convinced about Paisley's idea.

"A tres leches ice cream cake could win the bake sale award," Paisley said. "Do you know how delicious that would be?"

Newton chattered again, as if he agreed.

Ben patted his stomach. "Be that as it may, what about the rules and what if the ice cream melts?"

"Sure, it will be more challenging, but more likely to win us the award. We'll make it work," Paisley said.

Newton climbed from Paisley's shoulder up Ben's arm. Newton's ticklish claws made him laugh.

"I'll think about it," Ben said.

Paisley had to figure out how to convince Ben. She

would keep it in the back of her mind, but for now, the two of them focused on studying the bacteria specimen.

Under Dad's high-power microscope, the yellow goo looked more like little crabs sitting on the fibers of a dust mitt. Paisley knew better, but she was kind of disappointed. She expected to see little green alien men and women instead.

"Bacteria are the oldest living things on Earth and possibly lots of other places. Life depends on bacteria," Dad said.

Ben took a look next. "What is that black spot?" he asked.

Dad focused the microscope. "Hmm. I don't know."

It always surprised Paisley when her dad wasn't sure about something.

"A scientist named Bonnie Bessler gave a good talk about how bacteria communicate using chemical signals. I need to research more, but perhaps this is the case here," Dad said.

Paisley couldn't wait to see the bacteria under the high-power microscope again. When it was her turn, her eyes took a moment to adjust. Then she saw the black spot that Ben noticed.

Paisley magnified the microscope to get an even better look at the spot.

Weird!

The spot looked like a game controller. It was oval with a toggle.

Her imagination had a tendency to run wild sometimes, so she wanted to get a second opinion.

"Ben, don't move a single thing and take another look. Tell me what this looks like," Paisley said.

"Is it a controller of some sorts?" Ben asked.

Paisley couldn't contain her excitement and jumped up. She almost knocked the microscope and petri dish over.

"Careful," Dad said. "The specimen is precious and so is the microscope."

Even Dad agreed that the spot looked like a controller when he took a look. What on Earth or elsewhere did it mean? Dad talked some more about the way bacteria communicate in chemical words,

especially when they gathered in groups. Did this controller-like thing have anything to do with bacteria communication or transportation?

Paisley couldn't wait to talk to Ben alone. Newton seemed to sense her excitement and ran around in a circle.

Chapter Three
Spelling Bee Catastrophe

Paisley walked Ben home, which wasn't far at all. Ben had calculated that their homes were only fifteen-and-a-quarter feet apart.

"Please change your mind about the ice cream," Paisley begged.

"I think I know where you're going with this," Ben said.

Of course he probably did. Ben and Paisley had been friends since they were both in diapers.

"I have a feeling we can get the ingredients for our

out-of-this-world treat from out of this world," Paisley said.

"You think it will work? What about the rules?" Ben asked.

Paisley knew she had him hooked. "Everything will be fine," she said, and hoped she would be right. "We can at least give it a try. We'll have fun no matter what."

"I'll think about it some more. At least the fun part seems to be a guarantee," Ben said.

All night, Paisley dreamed about little green men and women flying on meteorites. She didn't want the dream to end and she didn't want to get ready for school when she awoke the next morning, either.

It was the day of Whitney-Raelynn's city-wide spelling bee. The bake sale would take place the day after. If Whitney-Raelynn won both, Paisley was sure all of Roarington Elementary would never hear the end of it.

She was right. When Whitney-Raelynn arrived at school that day, she wore a green shirt layered over a white shirt that had four blocks: "Ge. Ni. U. S." Genius, written out in the periodic elements (Ge = germanium, Ni = Nickel. U = Uranium, and S = Sulphur).

It would've been Paisley's new favorite shirt had anyone worn it other than Whitney-Raelynn. In fact, Paisley wished she could give a shirt like that to her mom to celebrate the new research.

"I might be the Grammar Girl, but I'm great in science, too," Whitney-Raelynn said.

"Grammar Grinch is more like it," Paisley said under her breath.

Paisley might've said something else, but Ben steered her to the gym to throw some hoops before school started. "Just ignore her," he said.

Paisley had a hard time ignoring Whitney-Raelynn when she kept bragging to everyone that she was going to win the city and state competition.

"You should've been the one going to the city competition, Ben," Paisley said.

Ben shrugged his shoulders. He took a break to eat some of the sacked lunch he brought from home. That

was his second breakfast and Paisley wondered if he packed a second lunch in there, too.

"Be that as it may, I'm glad I didn't miss an exciting adventure to help out your mom," Ben said.

"Thanks for being such a good friend," Paisley said.

"I've been thinking," Ben said, drawing out a pause so long it nearly drove Paisley crazy. "An out-of-this-world tres leche ice cream cake is a wonderful idea."

Paisley whooped and ran around in a circle just like Newton would have if a mongoose were allowed in school. "You're the best, Ben," she said.

Paisley had a hard time concentrating for the rest of the day, even in science class when Mrs. Beaker gave them another free period. She brought out measuring cups and chemistry kits for practice. Ben created a snow cone solution.

The PTA meeting and bake sale would be held the next night and Paisley kept brainstorming. After school, she wanted to prepare but she also couldn't miss the spelling bee at The Music Hall of

Roarington.

Mrs. Proton offered extra credit to encourage students to support Whitney-Raelynn. Paisley thought of herself as supporting Roarington Elementary instead. Extra credit was always nice.

During the spelling bee breaks, Paisley chatted with Ben about ingredients that they would need for the cake. They needed cream, evaporated milk, condensed milk, cake mix, and other items to make ice cream. "What if we found the salt and the ice for the ice cream from a different galaxy? The treat will be much tastier and people will pay a ton more!"

Ben stared off in the distance as if he was imagining it. "That would be awesome!"

The spelling bee got more interesting when Whitney-Raelynn stood on stage. "Hi," she said into the microphone.

The acoustics of the music hall had improved after Paisley and Ben solved a sound mystery there. The lights were so bright that Paisley could barely read Whitney-Raelynn's "Genius" shirt. She doubted anyone else could read it either, which kind of made her happy.

Whitney-Raelynn had been taking voice-projection classes and she sounded extra confident as she spelled her way through several rounds. Paisley couldn't wait for the spelling bee to end so she and Ben could get to their lab and tinker in the kitchen.

"Can you spell ochidore?" the judge said to Whitney-Raelynn a while later. "Ochidore. A type of crab. The ochidore swim on the shore."

Paisley nearly flew out of the wooden seat. The ochidore looked just like the bacteria specimen! Ben leaned forward. They both had to keep themselves from shouting out the correct spelling. It paid having scientists for parents.

Whitney-Raelynn's confident smile fell. "O-c-c-o-d-a-r," she said into the microphone.

"I'm sorry," the judge said. "The correct spelling is o-c-h-i-d-o-r-e."

Paisley thought this would've been a moment of triumph to see Whitney-Raelynn defeated in front

of so many students and teachers, including Mrs. Proton. Instead, Paisley's stomach hurt as she watched Whitney-Raelynn tear up.

It really would've been great if a Roarington Elementary student had won the spelling bee, and maybe the school could've gotten even more money for equipment. Sure, Paisley and Ben deserved the chance to be there, but Whitney-Raelynn had followed the rules, showed up when she needed to, and worked hard.

Whitney-Raelynn peeled off her outer shirt layer, tossed it to the ground, and stomped on the word "genius."

Paisley raced over to pick the shirt up. She tried handing it back to Whitney-Raelynn.

"I'm too loser-tastic to wear a shirt like that now."

"You don't have to be a winner to be a genius," Paisley said. Had those words really come out of her mouth?

"You keep it," Whitney-Raelynn.

Paisley wasn't sure what to do with it. The shirt

was way too little for Mom anyway.

Ben smiled at Paisley as she stuffed Whitney-Raelynn's shirt into her backpack. "You tried your best," he said.

Paisley shrugged. Her mind and heart felt heavy as she walked home. At least they had an exciting experiment and bake sale to prepare for.

Chapter Four
Alpha Centauri!

Newton greeted Paisley and Ben with cornmeal all over his nose. The kitchen was still a disaster from the night before.

"We'll deal with this later," Paisley said.

"We better or we won't have anywhere to prepare our ice cream cake," Ben said. He pulled out a few clean pots and pans to get ready.

Dad was busy on a conference call and Paisley didn't want to disturb him. She slipped into his office and borrowed the petri dish.

"What are we supposed to do with it?" Ben asked when she brought it into the kitchen.

Paisley wasn't quite sure. "I think we need to connect the key to the controller somehow." She removed the outer protective case and then pressed the key flat against the petri dish. "Please take us to get ingredients from a different galaxy," she requested.

Paisley bumped her fist against Ben's and they chanted, "Science Alliance!"

Nothing seemed to happen at first. Then Paisley began to shake all over. Was an earthquake about to hit Roarington?

Ben must've felt it as well because he reached for the pots and pans. Newton squealed and ran off.

An instant later, the pots and pans turned into protective suits of armor protecting Paisley and Ben. They beamed into the air.

The bacteria in the petri dish glowed neon yellow, lighting the atmosphere. "To Alpha Centauri," a strange voice said.

Was that code for something? The toggle increased

in size and the lid of the petri dish disappeared.

They traveled at such a fast speed that Paisley could barely take a breath let alone laugh the way she wanted to. This had to be the most exciting mode of transportation EVER!

Paisley and Ben arrived in the closest galaxy to Earth. Now the name Alpha Centauri made sense. The pull of gravity sent them in orbit in this neighboring star system.

"Alpha Centauri is more than four light-years away. I can't believe we got here in an instant!" Ben said. His voice sounded funny.

So did Paisley's when she tried to speak. "Check out the incredible sights," she said. Her mind was blown as she looked around.

Molten lava flared from a star much like the sun, only bigger and brighter. As Paisley and Ben orbited by at a distance, their suits warmed.

The second star was slightly smaller, but together, the stars reminded Paisley of the twins Suki and Sumi. When Paisley saw these two stars in the night sky at

her house, they always appeared like one. She'd never imagined she'd get a chance to see them up close like this.

A third red dwarf star glowed so far off in the sky that Paisley almost thought she was imagining it.

"Planets!" Paisley shouted a few moments later.

Ben didn't have his field journal with him or else he might've started drawing. Paisley wished she had a camera to record the planets since even powerful telescopes had trouble studying Alpha Centauri.

Ben made some calculations. "That planet is about the same size of Earth," he said.

Even though Paisley was warm from how close she was to the stars, she had the chills again thinking about what and who lived on those planets. Were there kids just like her and Ben? Paisley started to get caught up in the dazzling sights and her curiosity about what other kids in this solar system might look or act like. Did they have things like spelling bees and bake sales?

At the thought of the bake sale, Paisley remembered their mission. They would need ice and salt, which would lower the freezing point of the ice cream.

"Let's go check out the Earth-like planet," Paisley said. The toggle glowed red as they traveled toward it.

"We will burn up in a millisecond if we land there!" Ben said.

Paisley's skin burned even in the suit. "Retreat!" she yelled and tried to move the toggle.

They beamed somewhere in the star system that was unfamiliar to both Paisley and Ben. It wasn't so hot in this region. They were safe. For now, at least.

They orbited by a planet that looked like a twin to the other one, only this planet appeared to have polar caps. The toggle's color changed to blue.

"Ice!" Paisley said and moved the toggle. "Let's land here to gather some resources."

Paisley shivered when they landed on the planet. The pots and pan suit might've shielded them, but it wasn't warm.

"I wish I could draw all of these spectacular details," Ben said as they walk-bounced on the planet because of the strange gravity.

Towers of ice surrounded a sea. If there was water,

then there could be life! Paisley didn't see any living things though, especially not little green men and women.

Ben stored some ice in one of the baking pans linked to his armor. Paisley did the same.

Salt was easy enough to find. It was dissolved in the water when Ben inspected it. When the ice froze, it forced most of the salt out. How were they going to store the salty water, though? There wasn't storage space left on their suits unless they got rid of ice they collected.

What about the empty petri dish Paisley held?

WAIT—EMPTY?

"Where did the toggle and the bacteria specimen go?" she cried out.

Ben pointed at a mustard glow in saltwater. The bacteria specimen along with the toggle escaped. The glow flashed a rainbow of colors before it completely disappeared.

"I think it just said goodbye to us," Paisley said, her teeth chattering from the cold.

"The bacteria must live here," Ben said. His teeth

chattered, too.

Paisley liked the idea of the bacteria returning home instead of being stuck in a petri dish forever, but what did that mean for her and Ben? Were they going to be icicles on this planet that they didn't even have a name for? Would future scientists find them and wonder how human life got there?

"We'll start experiencing frostbite in approximately seven minutes," Ben said.

Seven minutes!

They were going to freeze on a strange planet in Alpha Centauri if they couldn't get home fast.

Paisley missed her mom more than she ever had, plus her dad and of course, Newton. Winning the bake sale award no longer seemed like a big deal.

Chapter Five
You Don't Have to Be a Winner to be a Genius

Paisley watched as the salty water flashed yellow in several spots at once. She remembered what Dad had said about bacteria communicating together when they were in groups.

"You think this is turning into a welcome home party?" Paisley asked.

Ben trembled as he counted down the seconds until they got frostbite and froze to death. "I want our own welcome home party."

Paisley did, too. There was no way she could find

the exact bacteria specimen in this huge body of water. If she'd been stuck in a petri dish or in a meteorite, she'd want to be free, too.

"We thank you for getting us here. It has been amazing and we've learned a lot, but we'd like to return to Earth," Paisley said above the salt water. Even if Whitney-Raelynn wasn't here to witness this, Paisley still felt silly. It was a matter of life and death, though. She dipped her key in the water and hoped it activated a bacteria toggle communicator.

Paisley barely had time to dip the petri dish in the salt water before they were beamed once again. She couldn't breathe.

Would they return to their solar system? Back on Earth? In her house?

Paisley and Ben returned to the middle of some pantry. They were so dizzy that they knocked a shelf of food down and fell on a large bag of flour, splitting it open. A flour cloud filled the air.

They could barely get up until they took off their pot and pan suits. The ice had started to melt, but it had survived the lightning fast journey. The petri dish full of salt water had, too, though some spilled on Paisley's feet.

Just when Paisley wondered if they were in the right pantry, Newton burst in and climbed up to her shoulder. Seeing Newton always made her smile, but never this much.

"I can't believe it," Ben said.

Dad said the same thing a moment later when he walked into the kitchen.

Flour was all over the floor. The pots and pans were warped and scorched. Plus, it was still a mess from last night's dinner.

"Where in there world have you two been and where is the bacteria specimen?" Dad asked.

"Actually, we've been out of this world," Paisley said, filling him on their adventures.

"That bacteria specimen was priceless," Dad said. "You shouldn't borrow something without asking first. I think you did the right thing, though. This salt and the water will likely give us even more information and you freed the bacteria." Dad didn't quite do his air-guitar dance, but he muttered to himself, "Planets and life in Alpha Centauri. Unbelievable."

Paisley and Ben were exhausted from their trip, but they had to get ready for the bake sale. They did their best to come up with something to bring.

A tres leches ice cream cake no longer seemed like a good idea. The pans were in bad shape and the flour bag was empty. Newton looked like a snow weasel the way he kept sliding in the flour.

"We can still make the ice cream," Ben said.

"I think we should make tres leches frozen yogurt instead," Paisley said. "Yogurt has bacteria in it. We owe a lot to bacteria."

"This is my favorite idea for the bake sale yet," Ben said. He helped Paisley mix cream, vanilla yogurt, and a caramel sauce together. The hardest part was trying to keep Ben from eating the ingredients.

They put the milky mix into a plastic bag and sealed it. Then they set it into a bigger bag with the Alpha Centauri ice and salt water mix.

They had just the right amount of ice and salt. Maybe Paisley imagined it, but the solution seemed to glow the slightest bit yellow. Even Newton helped them tumble the bags around until the yogurt froze. The cold reminded Paisley and Ben of the frozen mountains on the strange planet.

"We should name the planet something," Ben said.

Paisley liked Ben's idea, even if future scientists weren't aware of it or if the aliens on the planet called it something else. "How about Planet Pabe?"

"Why Pabe?" Ben asked.

"The first two letters of both of our names."

Ben's smile told Paisley he approved.

As soon as the yogurt was ready, Dad moved the salty, icy solution to his lab for proper storage. "I can't wait to study this," he said.

Mom said the same thing when Paisley checked in with her. While Mom couldn't join the PTA meeting in person, Paisley at least felt she was a part of things.

"Good luck tonight, *mija*," Mom said. "And you better clean up that chaotic kitchen."

Mom was right about the kitchen chaos. Cleaning would come soon, but first, the PTA meeting!

Dad helped Paisley and Ben set their frozen yogurt on dry ice before he drove them and Ben's parents to the PTA meeting. They brought some recyclable bowls and spoons.

The bake sale was already under way and many of the fifth graders had awesome displays to go with their treats.

Arjun made an Indian dessert called Sandesh and created a map to go along with it.

Suki and Sumi created a model of the peanut to go with their treat. Arjun fortunately didn't have any allergic reactions.

Rosalind baked daredevil chocolate brownies with peppers.

Whitney-Raelynn had done an amazing job. No surprise! She had crushed a bunch of graham crackers to look like a sandy shore. She'd carved crabs out of crispy rice cereal marshmallow bites and set them on the "sand." Blue raspberry cupcakes lined the crushed graham crackers to look like an ocean.

"Ochidore," Paisley said when she saw the display.

"I know how to spell it now, even if I'm loser-tastic," Whitney-Raelynn said.

"A loser could not have created this or gotten so far in the spelling bee," Paisley said. She dug the Genius shirt out of her backpack and returned it to Whitney-Raelynn.

Paisley wasn't sure what Whitney-Raelynn would do with the shirt, but she almost smiled at her when she put the shirt on over the other one she was wearing.

"Thanks," she said quietly.

The bake sale treats sold out quickly, even Rosalind's spicy brownies, though not everyone dared eat them. Paisley and Ben sold out the quickest thanks to their exotic ingredients. They raised ten times more money than any other entry.

Everyone talked about how delicious and unique the tres leches frozen yogurt tasted. That made them even more surprised when Mrs. Proton slipped Paisley and Ben a piece of paper that read, "Disqualified."

If Paisley had paid attention to the rules, she would've known that to be eligible for the bake sale award, the item had to be baked.

Oh well. The award was nothing compared to the reward of making the treat with Ben, especially gathering the alien ingredients together.

Not a single person was surprised when Whitney-Raelynn won the bake sale award. Well, except for Arjun because he thought Whitney-Raelynn should be disqualified for making both crispy treats *and* cupcakes.

"You don't have to be a winner to be a genius," Whitney-Raelynn whispered to Paisley before accepting the award.

Paisley smiled even if she would never hear the end of Whitney-Raelynn's bake sale victory. She felt grateful she and Ben arrived alive at the PTA meeting. Maybe they'd get a chance to see their neighboring galaxy again with the school's new super-powered telescope.

Science Alliance!
Yummy Frozen Yogurt Fun

You'll Need:

- measuring cups and spoons
- 2 tablespoons (30 ml) coconut milk
- ½ cup (120 ml) vanilla yogurt (regular or low-fat)
- 1 tablespoon (15 ml) caramel sauce for a tres leches twist (optional)
- ¼ teaspoon (1.25 ml) vanilla extract
- ½ cup (120 ml) rock salt
- 2 cups (480 ml) ice
- 1-quart (.95 ml) zip top bag
- 1-gallon (3.8 ml) zip top bag

Directions:

1. Add caramel sauce, coconut milk, vanilla yogurt, and vanilla extract to the quart zip top bag. Zip the bag tightly.
2. Put that bag into the gallon zip top bag.
3. Add rock salt to the gallon zip top bag of ice.
4. Place the sealed quart bag inside gallon bag full of ice and rock salt. Carefully seal the gallon bag.
5. Holding the edges (or using a towel or gloves), shake the gallon bag from side to side for at least five minutes until the liquid freezes into a solid. The more you shake, the better the yogurt will freeze.
6. Open and enjoy!

Women in Science

Bonnie Bassler is a molecular biologist. She said that a human has about thirty thousand genes, but there are about one-hundred more times bacterial genes in our bodies. These genes play a big role in our lives. "I know you think of yourself as human beings, but I think of you as ninety or ninety-nine percent bacterial," Bonnie Bassler said.

Bonnie Bassler (b. 1962)

Author Q & A

Q: If you could travel anywhere in space, where would you go?

A: I would love to see the rings of Jupiter up close and of course explore Alpha Centauri.

Q: Have you ever had any kitchen disasters?

A: I once forgot to add sugar to a cake recipe. I've also burned a few dishes in my day.

Q: What about writing disasters?

A: My computer crashed and I lost an entire novel I'd been working on and had to rewrite it from scratch.

Silly Science!

Q: What's in an astronaut's favorite sandwich?

A: Launch meat.

Q: Why did the cow travel to outer space?

A: To get to the Milky Way.

Q: How do astronauts like to serve dinner?

A: On flying saucers.

Websites to Visit

For more information about galaxies:

*science.nasa.gov/astrophysics/focus-areas/
  what-are-galaxies*

To learn more about space:

www.nasa.gov/audience/forkids/kidsclub/flash

For information about Alpha Centauri:

*imagine.gsfc.nasa.gov/features/cosmic/
  nearest_star_info.html*

About the Author

J.L. Anderson's education inspired her to become an author, but she thought seriously about becoming a biologist, and she once was the president of the science club in high school. She lives outside of Austin, Texas with her husband, daughter, and two naughty dogs. You can learn more about her at www.jessicaleeanderson.com.

About the Illustrator

Alan Brown's love of comic art, cartoons and drawing has driven him to follow his dreams of becoming an artist. His career as a freelance artist and designer has allowed him to work on a wide range of projects, from magazine illustration and game design to children's books. He's had the good fortune to work on comics such as *Ben 10* and *Bravest Warriors*. Alan lives in Newcastle with his wife, sons and dog.